COULD YOU SURVIVE
THE JURASSIC PERIOD?
AN INTERACTIVE PREHISTORIC ADVENTURE

BY MATT DOEDEN · ILLUSTRATED BY JUAN CALLE

Content Consultant: Mathew Wedel, PhD
Associate Professor, Department of Anatomy
Western University of Health Sciences

You Choose Books are published by Capstone Press, an imprint of Capstone.
1710 Roe Crest Drive
North Mankato, Minnesota 56003
www.capstonepub.com

Library of Congress Cataloging-in-Publication Data
Names: Doeden, Matt, author. | Calle, Juan, illustrator. Title: Could you survive
the Jurassic period? : an interactive prehistoric adventure / by Matt Doeden ;
illustrated by Juan Calle. Description: North Mankato, Minnesota : Capstone
Press, [2020] | Series: You choose: prehistoric survival | Includes bibliographical
references and index. | Audience: Ages 8-11. | Audience: Grades 4-6. | Summary:
The reader's choices determine whether three friends will survive after being
mysteriously transported back in time to when huge insects swarmed the skies
and fearsome dinosaurs ruled. Identifiers: LCCN 2019044975 (print) | LCCN
2019044976 (ebook) | ISBN 9781543574029 (hardcover) | ISBN 9781496658081
(paperback) | ISBN 9781543574074 (pdf) Subjects: LCSH: Plot-your-own stories.
| CYAC: Dinosaurs--Fiction. | Prehistoric animals--Fiction. | Time travel--Fiction.
| Paleontology--Fiction. | Adventure and adventurers--Fiction. | Plot-your-own
stories. Classification: LCC PZ7.D692 Csj 2020 (print) | LCC PZ7.D692 (ebook) |
DDC [Fic]--dc23 LC record available at https://lccn.loc.gov/2019044975 LC ebook
record available at https://lccn.loc.gov/2019044976

Summary: Text leads readers through a Jurassic Period adventure in which they can
choose what to do and where to go next.

Photo Credits
Design Elements: Capstone and Shutterstock: Art studio G, Miceking, tinkivinki

Editorial Credits
Editor: Mandy Robbins; Designer: Bobbie Nyutten; Media Researcher: Jo Miller;
Production Specialist: Tori Abraham

Printed and bound in the United States of America.
3184

TABLE OF CONTENTS

INTRODUCTION

YOU are an ordinary kid going about your everyday life. Suddenly you find yourself in a strange place and a strange time. It's a period from long ago. The world looks different than anything you've ever seen before. Terrifying beasts roam the land. Danger lurks at every turn. Where will you find shelter? How will you get food? Will you ever see your friends and family again? Most importantly of all, can you survive?

Chapter One sets the scene. Then you choose which path to take. Follow the directions at the bottom of each page. The choices you make determine what happens next. After you finish your path, go back and read the others for more adventures.

YOU CHOOSE the path you take through the Jurassic Period!

Turn the page to begin your adventure.

CHAPTER 1

LOST IN TIME

"Look at that!" gasps your friend Eduardo.

He's pointing toward a huge Stegosaurus fossil on display at the science museum.

"Can you imagine running into one of those? Man, I wish I could see one in real life!"

"Boring," says Jasmine. "Where's the T. rex? I want to see a *real* dinosaur!"

Eduardo's face turns red. When it comes to dinosaurs, he's a fanatic. He fights the urge to snap at Jasmine as he grips the thick *Guide to the Jurassic* he bought at the gift shop.

"Jasmine," he says. "The sign says 'Jurassic Period.' Tyrannosaurus rex didn't live during the Jurassic, no matter what the movies say."

Turn the page.

"Hey," you say, glancing over your shoulder. "Our class is headed toward the Ancient Egypt exhibit. We should . . . "

Eduardo cuts you off. "Just a second. Check this out!"

The three of you step up to the base of the Stegosaurus skeleton. "Put your hand on it."

"I don't think we're supposed to touch it," Jasmine warns.

"Nobody's looking," Eduardo responds. "Imagine what the world must have been like."

All three of you touch the fossil. It's smooth and cool to the touch. You imagine what this animal would have looked like when it was alive.

Suddenly a wave of dizziness sweeps over you. Your stomach churns. You feel like you're falling. Then everything goes black.

When you regain consciousness, something is wrong. The museum is gone. You're outside, lying in a sunbaked clearing. Tall trees and strange ferns grow all around you. The air smells damp.

Eduardo wakes up next to you, his book still clutched under his arm. And there's Jasmine, just starting to sit up and rub her eyes.

"What . . . where?" Eduardo stammers.

None of this makes any sense. You look up. The sky is brilliant blue, dotted with clouds.

A shadow passes overhead. Is it a bird? It's huge! You squint your eyes and scream. A creature soars high above—a creature that should not be there.

"It's . . . it's . . . a pterosaur!" Eduardo gasps.

"This can't be possible," Jasmine says. "It can't be real!"

Turn the page.

Far in the distance, you hear a low roaring sound. Some sort of animal made it. And from the sound of it, it's a *huge* animal. That, combined with the strange plant life and the pterosaur in the sky, leaves no doubt of what has happened, no matter how insane it sounds.

"Umm, Eduardo," you whisper. "I don't think we have to imagine the Jurassic anymore. I'm afraid we're in it."

You stand at the edge of a dense forest, which lies to your north. The land east and south drops off into what looks like a large wetland area. An open prairie covered with ferns lies to the west.

"Where do we go?" Eduardo asks.

"You're the dinosaur expert," Jasmine snaps. "Why don't you tell us?"

Both of them look at you. Someone has to make a decision.

To head into the forest, turn to page 13.
To venture out onto the prairie, turn to page 49.
To wade into the wetlands, turn to page 79.

CHAPTER 2

THE PREHISTORIC FOREST

As another bone-chilling roar rolls over the land, you suddenly feel very exposed.

"Let's take cover in the forest!" you shout.

The three of you rush toward the thick trees and bushes. Huge ferns slap at your face as you charge into the brush. The branches of large pine trees hang low, forcing you to duck and weave as you run. Jasmine stumbles over a tree root but pops right back up to her feet. The farther in you go, the thicker the brush gets. Small flies swarm all over.

Your heart races when Eduardo suddenly screams. Is it a dinosaur?

Turn the page.

"It's huge! Get it away! Get it away!" he shouts, swatting at the air.

Then you see it. An enormous bug that looks like a dragonfly buzzes around his face.

"Wow, it's as long as my arm!" Jasmine gasps.

You've never seen anything like it. Eduardo keeps shouting, trying to swat the insect away. It finally buzzes away deeper into the forest.

"Aw, Ed, be nice. He's just welcoming us to the Jurassic," Jasmine says with a nervous laugh.

You start giggling, too. Then she laughs some more. Which makes you laugh even harder. Eduardo just scowls.

"If you two are ready to stop being ridiculous," Eduardo says, "I'd remind you that we're trapped in the past and surrounded by creatures that probably want to eat us."

Of course, he's right. It's so absurd that laughing is almost all you can do.

"OK," you say, calming yourself. "Let's think. We'll need food."

"And shelter," Eduardo suggests.

"I'm thirsty," Jasmine says. "We're going to need water before anything else."

To search for shelter, turn the page.
To look for food and water, turn to page 19.

"We need to find somewhere safe," you decide. "Let's look for shelter."

Ahead, the land rises into rolling hills. Eduardo suggests that maybe you can find a cave or a narrow canyon in that direction. Getting there won't be easy, though. The forest is dense. You scramble through thick brush and trees for what seems like an hour. When you finally find a large clearing, it's filled with the most amazing creatures you've ever seen. You hang back in the trees, staring.

"Brachiosaurus!" Eduardo says. "Look at them! They make an elephant look tiny."

The huge beasts lumber through the clearing, munching on trees. They're fantastic. And luckily, they don't pay you any attention. The only bad thing about them is the smell. It reminds you of a cattle barn.

Turn the page.

"This isn't a safari," Jasmine says. "We can't just stop and take in the sights. Let's give them plenty of room and keep going."

"Are you kidding?" Eduardo says. "We're the only humans to have ever seen these animals in real life! We have to get a closer look. And take some pictures!"

To keep going and move around the Brachiosauruses, turn to page 32.

To get a closer look at the Brachiosauruses, turn to page 42.

Jasmine is right. All that running has left you feeling thirsty, and your stomach is already beginning to rumble.

"We can't do anything if we're dying of thirst and hunger," you decide. "This is a forest. It should be loaded with things we can eat."

The three of you move across the forest floor, scanning for food.

"Where are all the flowers?" Jasmine asks. "Shouldn't they be blooming everywhere?"

"There were no flowers in the Jurassic," Eduardo says. "They hadn't evolved yet."

"I guess that means no gigantic bees to worry about then," Jasmine says. "That's good news."

"But no flowers means no fruit," you point out. "That makes our food search more difficult."

Turn the page.

"Look at that," Jasmine says, pointing to the ground. "Animal tracks!"

Sure enough, a set of small tracks leads toward a stand of pine trees. If there's no fruit, maybe you can find some meat to eat.

"Hold on," Eduardo says. "I hear the sound of running water. There could be a stream."

To follow the animal tracks, go to the next page.
To look for the source of the running water,
turn to page 22.

"Maybe it's something we can eat," you say, looking at the tracks.

Reluctantly, Eduardo agrees to follow the tracks with you and Jasmine. You follow them along a muddy stretch of forest floor, right up to a small tree.

"Look," Jasmine says, pointing at a branch.

There, munching on a seed, sits a furry little . . . something. It's about the size of a squirrel, but longer and leaner. It looks at you with brown eyes, curious, but not afraid. It's a mammal.

Jasmine reaches for a large rock. She raises the rock over her head as she slowly approaches the small animal.

"Here goes nothing," she says. "Sorry little fella', but we need food."

To tell Jasmine to stop, turn to page 24.
To continue the hunt, turn to page 34.

"A stream? That means water!" you say.

The three of you tromp through the forest to a small stream. The water rushes toward a larger river beyond. On the far bank, you see several large Ceratosauruses, but they don't notice you.

"Eduardo, were there fish in the Jurassic Period?" you ask.

"Of course," he says. "Fish evolved long before land creatures. This river might be full of them."

You smile. "Well then, I think we've just found our source of both food *and* water."

"We should make camp here," Jasmine says.

Eduardo nods. "Maybe. It would keep us close to food and water. Of course, other animals would want to stay close too. That could be a problem."

To suggest a different spot to make camp, turn to page 27.
To set up a camp near the river, turn to page 43.

"Jasmine, don't do it!" you cry.

At the sound of your voice, the little mammal scurries away up the tree.

"What was that?" Jasmine asks with a scowl.

"Think about it," you say. "We're mammals. What if that was an ancient ancestor?"

"Don't be ridiculous," Jasmine snaps at you, tossing the rock aside. "Now we're all going to go hungry."

"I don't think so," Eduardo interrupts. He's munching on a handful of seeds. "Look, these are what that little animal was eating. They're not bad!"

He's right. The seeds aren't bad, and they're everywhere. The three of you eat your fill, feeling stronger by the moment.

Then you hear a rustling sound from behind you. Slowly, you turn around. A dinosaur emerges into the clearing, about a football field's distance from where you stand. The animal is as long as a pickup truck and walks on two legs. Its razor-sharp teeth gleam in the sunlight that trickles through to the forest floor.

"Ceratosaurus," Eduardo whispers. "Predator."

The dinosaur hasn't seen you yet. It's sniffing at the air, possibly confused by your unfamiliar scent. You suddenly feel like the small mammal Jasmine was about to kill.

To remain still and silent, turn the page.
To run, turn to page 35.

"Don't move," you whisper.

You watch the huge beast out of the corner of your eye. The dinosaur takes a few steps in your direction. Its head moves slowly back and forth as it sniffs the air. Your heart races.

It's going to see us! you think. Your hands are shaking. Your knees are about to buckle. You're doomed!

Just when you can't take it anymore, something rushes out of the brush. It's a small reptile. The Ceratosaurus springs into action, chasing the reptile into the forest.

"Phew!" Jasmine gasps. All three of you collapse to the forest floor.

"We're never going to be safe here, are we?" Eduardo asks.

Turn to page 33.

"I don't think that's a good idea," you argue, pointing at the Ceratosaurus on the far bank. "All kinds of animals use this river as a source of food and water. If we stay here, we'll just be another item on the menu for predators."

"Hmm, good point," Eduardo says. "Let's collect some water and look somewhere else for a place to camp."

Luckily, Jasmine has a large, stainless-steel water bottle. You'll need to boil the water to make it safe to drink, but it's a perfect opportunity to fill it. You could fill it in this small trickle of water and stay hidden, or you could risk going to the river to fill it faster.

To fill it from the small stream, turn the page.
To go to the bank of the large river to fill it, turn to page 40.

"Let's stay away from the main river for now," you suggest. "There's no way of knowing what might be lurking there."

Jasmine slowly fills the bottle in the small stream, and you make your way deeper into the forest. As you move along the forest floor, you can't help but feel like it's only a matter of time before some Jurassic beast spots you and decides to see how you taste. Meanwhile, Jasmine collects cones from the forest's dense pine trees.

"Pine nuts," she says. "We can eat these!"

The nuts don't taste very good, and they're a lot of work to get, but at least it's something. It gives you confidence you'll find more things to eat as you explore. You move along a rocky ridge. In the distance, you spot several openings.

"Look, caves," you say. "They're perfect!"

"Umm, there's a small problem," Jasmine interrupts. "Actually a huge problem!"

Between you and the caves stands the biggest dinosaur you've seen yet. It has a body the size of a bulldozer, a broad tail, and a long neck. Instinctively, you start to back up.

"Wait," Eduardo says. "It's eating plants. I think it's some sort of sauropod. If we give it some space, it's not going to care about us."

You look back at the beast. If Eduardo is wrong, you'll all be dinosaur food.

To move around the sauropod to the cave, turn the page.

To turn around, turn to page 39.

It will be dark soon, and you don't want to be trapped out here when the sun sets.

"OK, slowly then," you say.

The three of you carefully sneak across the clearing. The sauropod munches away on a tree, paying no attention to you at all. The three of you rush into the cave, falling to the floor with relief.

It's a small cave, but the narrow opening will protect you from larger predators. There are signs that some other animal once made its home here, but luckily the cave appears to be abandoned now. You have the uneasy feeling that this little cave might be home now.

Turn to page 33.

As much as you would love to watch the giant beasts, you need to find shelter before sundown. You give the enormous dinosaurs plenty of room as you move around them. Once you reach the tree-covered hills, you find exactly what you're looking for—some small caves.

"They're perfect," Jasmine says. "No predators are going to get us here."

You're exhausted. You collapse in one of the caves and fall asleep. When you wake, you're sure it was all a dream. But no. You're still here, lying in a dusty cave, 150 million years in the past.

Go to the next page.

Every day is a struggle for survival. Over time, you and your friends find sources of food and water. A small cave provides the perfect shelter from the Ceratosaurus, Torvosaurus, and other predators that roam the forest floor. You learn the patterns and movements of the dinosaurs and other Jurassic creatures. Slowly, you build a life in this strange time.

Years pass. As you grow into adulthood, you become restless. You dream of exploring more of the world. But the thought of leaving the only other human beings on the planet is terrifying.

You suggest striking out and leaving the forest. But Eduardo and Jasmine are determined to remain here, where they know they're somewhat safe.

To leave Eduardo and Jasmine to see the world, turn to page 36.

To remain safely in the hills, turn to page 46.

You hold your breath as Jasmine slams the rock with pinpoint accuracy. The animal never even tries to get away. But the moment it falls to the ground, you feel queasy. Your head spins. Beside you, Eduardo collapses to the ground. You and Jasmine both fall to your knees, grasping at your heads.

As you watch your friends, they seem to be fading away. It's almost like you can see right through them.

"Oh no," Eduardo says. "What have we done!"

"What?" gasps Jasmine. She's fading away.

"A mammal," Eduardo whispers. "You just killed one of our ancestors."

Your last thought as you fade away is that you may have just doomed the entire human race.

THE END

To follow another path, turn to page 11.
To learn more about the Jurassic Period, turn to page 103.

Your heart races. The Ceratosaurus sniffs again at the air. You can hear its huge claws scraping against rock.

As quickly as you can, you spring to your feet and start to sprint toward a thick stand of trees. The great predator screeches as it targets you. It's blindingly fast. You never even stood a chance. It knocks you to the ground with a sickening thud. The powerful impact knocks you out instantly. That's a good thing, because what comes next is much, much worse.

THE END

To follow another path, turn to page 11.
To learn more about the Jurassic Period, turn to page 103.

"I'm sorry," you tell your friends. "I just can't stay here anymore. I need to see what's out there. I really wish you would join me."

Eduardo just shakes his head. Jasmine frowns. With a hug for each, you say goodbye.

"I'll come back one day," you promise.

With that, you strike out on the adventure of a lifetime. You see a great Brontosaurus grazing. You walk with herds of Stegosauruses. You narrowly escape being eaten by a fierce Allosaurus, twice! You even gain a companion—a young Dryosaurus that seems to think you're its mother.

It's an experience unlike any other. Yet in the dark of night, you're lonely. During the days, you often find yourself gazing out to the horizon, wondering if your friends are still out there.

Turn the page.

Years later, you go back home. Your friends welcome you back with open arms and a surprise. Their little family of two has grown. They have a daughter, Kiara! It's a new life in an old time. But for the first time, this place and time finally feel like home.

THE END

To follow another path, turn to page 11.
To learn more about the Jurassic Period, turn to page 103.

"That dinosaur could crush a car," you say. "We can't risk it. Let's find some other shelter."

Eduardo shrugs and follows you. You walk for hours without finding shelter. The sun sets, and darkness falls over the forest.

"This is bad," Jasmine says.

The three of you nestle together against a large rock. Every snap and crunch on the forest floor makes your heart race. Then you hear a different sort of sound. It's a huffing sound . . . breathing. You scan for the source of it, but you can't see anything.

When the beast makes its charge, you have no chance. It's so dark you never even see what kind of dinosaur it is. The only good news is that the attack doesn't last long. Neither did your trip to the Jurassic.

THE END

To follow another path, turn to page 11.
To learn more about the Jurassic Period, turn to page 103.

"This stream is so shallow, it will be hard to fill the bottle," you say. "Let's try the river."

You navigate over rocks and mud to reach the river's bank. The water is a bit brown from sediment. Everything smells damp.

Jasmine hands you the bottle. You lower it into the river, letting the water flow inside.

"It's so peaceful here," you say. "I think this is going to be the perfect spot for—"

It all happens in an instant. An enormous shape bursts forth from the water. All you can see are jaws and teeth. You have just enough time to realize what it is—a giant crocodile—before it grabs you and drags you under the muddy water. Hopefully, Eduardo and Jasmine learn from your mistake.

THE END

To follow another path, turn to page 11.
To learn more about the Jurassic Period, turn to page 103.

"Come on!" Jasmine says, moving toward the grazing herd. She points to the phone you're carrying. "Take my picture with a dinosaur!"

You laugh. Jasmine carefully moves close to one of the huge beasts. She doesn't even come up to its knee. With a chuckle, you raise your phone.

"No wait!" Eduardo shouts—but not in time.

You press the button, and the camera clicks. The flash startles the Brachiosaurus. It raises up on its hind legs, then crashes back down to the ground. All of the giant dinosaurs begin to run.

It's a stampede! The huge dinosaurs crush everything in their path. You try to dart in between their legs but fail. A giant foot comes down, and the world goes black.

THE END

To follow another path, turn to page 11.
To learn more about the Jurassic Period, turn to page 103.

"There might not be any place in this world that's safe for us," you say. "This will have to do for now."

The three of you get to work building a camp. You use fallen branches to construct a small lean-to shelter. Over the next week, you master fishing. Eduardo manages to trap some small mammals and reptiles. You go into the forest collecting seeds and nuts. You hear large creatures in the forest several times, but you're lucky. None come near your camp.

One day, while you're fishing, something strange happens. The water begins to shimmer. It almost glows. Suddenly the reflection in the water is of another world. Your world! You shout for Jasmine and Eduardo, who rush to your side.

"It's home!" Jasmine shouts, then dives in.

Turn the page.

Just like that, she's gone. You and Eduardo are close behind. You dive into the cool water. When you emerge, the Jurassic is gone. It's replaced by familiar sights, sounds, and smells—buildings, car engines, and exhaust. You're on the side of a road. You don't know where you are exactly. But you know *when* you are. You can't wait to get back home.

THE END

To follow another path, turn to page 11.
To learn more about the Jurassic Period, turn to page 103.

You dare not venture out alone. This is home now. A few more years pass when Jasmine falls seriously ill with a fever.

"It was probably something she ate," Eduardo says. "Or something in the water."

Jasmine grows worse by the hour. With no modern medicine, there's nothing you can do for your friend but try to comfort her. She passes away in her sleep.

A month later, Eduardo goes out to collect food. He doesn't return. You go out to search for him the next day with no luck. As you're calling his name, something large stirs in the forest. You hear a roar.

You do the only thing you can. You run. Amazingly, you scramble back to your cave before the beast catches you.

You don't even know what kind of dinosaur it was. This is your life now. The rest of your days, however few they may be, will be spent as prey. And if the predators don't get you, starvation, dehydration, or illness will.

THE END

To follow another path, turn to page 11.
To learn more about the Jurassic Period, turn to page 103.

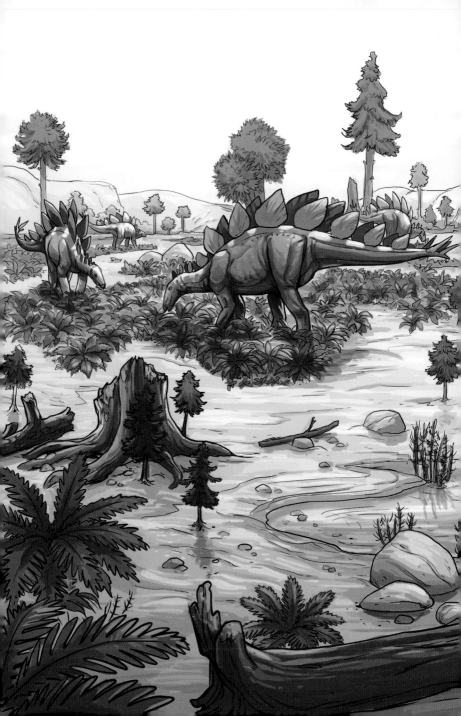

CHAPTER 3
THE OPEN PLAINS

"This way," you say, moving to the open prairie. "At least out here we'll be able to see anything big coming our way."

The plains seem to stretch on forever. Far in the distance, you can see a herd of some sort of dinosaurs grazing. "I think those are Stegosauruses," Eduardo says with excitement.

"Then let's steer clear," Jasmine suggests. "I don't want to be a Stegosaurus's lunch."

Eduardo laughs. "Don't be silly. They're herbivores. They wouldn't eat you any more than cows would eat you back home."

"Then let's go get a Stegosaurus burger," Jasmine jokes. "I'm hungry."

Turn the page.

Jasmine suddenly freezes. "What's that?" she says.

At first you don't see anything. Then something bursts out from the tall ferns. For a moment, you think it's a crow. It's about that size, and it's covered with feathers. But it's no crow. It looks like some crazy cross between a reptile and a bird.

"Archaeopteryx!" Eduardo squeals with delight.

"Well if I can't have a burger, I'll settle for some Jurassic chicken," Jasmine says.

"What?" Eduardo gasps with dismay. "How could you even think of it?"

"We need to eat," Jasmine answers.

The dinosaur looks at you curiously.

To try to hunt the Archaeopteryx, go to the next page.
To follow it, turn to page 53.

"Jasmine is right," you say. "We should take food when we can get it."

Eduardo looks at you both with disgust. He won't be any help.

"Jasmine, try to draw its attention," you say, "I'll grab it."

Jasmine starts to dance around, while you creep behind the dinosaur. You inch closer. You lunge, wrapping your arms around the animal. It lets out a screech and tries to break free. It's strong for its size, but you hold on tight. That's when it twists its neck and bites your hand.

You scream. The creature's powerful jaws clamp down on your fingers as your skin tears. Suddenly Jasmine dives at it. The little dinosaur lets go of your hand and darts back into the ferns.

Turn the page.

"Well that didn't go well," Eduardo says with a smirk.

"OK, OK. Let's not attack any more dinosaurs for a while," you agree.

Jasmine rips a strip of fabric from the bottom of her T-shirt and wraps your bleeding hand.

"Do you need a break, or are you ready to keep going?" Eduardo asks.

To press on in search of food and shelter, turn to page 62.
To find a place to rest, turn to page 72.

"No way," you whisper. "Did you see those sharp little teeth? Let's see where it goes."

You follow the strange creature as it wanders the open plains. Finally, it leads you back to a nest with six eggs.

"Jackpot!" Jasmine says.

When the dinosaur wanders away again, you grab three of the eggs. Eduardo piles some dry brush and focuses sunlight with his glasses, starting a small fire. You cook the eggs in the shells, then crack them open.

"Not bad," Jasmine says.

"I've been thinking," Eduardo says as he finishes his egg. "We got sent back here when we were imagining the Jurassic. Remember, we put our hands on the Stegosaurus skeleton? What if repeating that might bring us home?"

Turn the page.

"Worth a shot," Jasmine says. "Close your eyes. Imagine home."

You try to picture the museum in as much detail as you can. But when you open your eyes, you're still stuck in a prairie, 150 million years in the past.

"Maybe the Stegosaurus was the key," Jasmine jokes. Eduardo laughs.

But the comment gets you thinking. What if that *was* the key to whatever happened? Could you reproduce the effect?

To try to find somewhere safe to spend the night, turn the page.

To go in search of a Stegosaurus, turn to page 59.

"We need to be serious," you say. "The sun sets in a few hours. We don't want to be out here in the open when it does. We've got to find somewhere safe."

The prairie stretches on in every direction for what feels like forever. As exhaustion sets in, the three of you move along, single file, without speaking. The prospects for shelter are few.

"There are a few large rocks over there," Eduardo says. "We could hunker down there."

Jasmine points to a bushy tree on the horizon.

"We could climb to one of the higher limbs, out of reach of the predators."

The idea of sleeping in a tree isn't very appealing. But then, neither is being eaten by a dinosaur.

To head for the tree, go to the next page.
To take shelter by the rocks, turn to page 63.

You nod your head in agreement with Jasmine. "The tree seems like our best bet."

The sunset blazes brilliant orange by the time you reach the tree.

"I'll take this limb," Jasmine says, claiming the biggest, straightest limb.

You and Eduardo try to get comfortable in twisted crooks in the tree. It's a miserable night. A full moon shines brightly on the open plain.

"Is it just me, or does the moon seem bigger here?" Jasmine asks.

She's right. You'd swear the moon was bigger—or closer—here in the Jurassic. The moonlight shows the dark shapes of predators roaming the open plain. One of them approaches the tree.

"Allosaurus," Eduardo whispers. "Predator."

Turn the page.

Thankfully, you're far out of its reach, and it moves on.

"I'm *not* doing that again," Jasmine says as the three of you climb down in the morning. "Let's go find a Stegosaurus."

"Don't be ridiculous," you argue. "Last night proved how badly we need to find shelter.

Eduardo gives you a shrug. "Sorry, I'm with Jasmine. Let's go."

You watch as they head off in search of a Stegosaurus.

"Are you coming or what?" Jasmine calls.

To go with them, go to the next page.
To split up and continue the search for shelter, turn to page 66.

None of this makes sense. Why shouldn't you go in search of a Stegosaurus? It's as good a plan as any, and you can keep your eyes open for shelter while you look for a herd.

As the three of you move across the open plain, you try to process what has happened to you. None of this should be possible. How could a Stegosaurus fossil send you back in time? A squeal of delight from Jasmine interrupts your thoughts.

"There they are!" she cries.

There are hundreds of them. The Stegosauruses remind you of the bison you once saw at Yellowstone National Park. As you draw close to several stragglers in the herd, you begin to have second thoughts. These animals are *huge*. They're covered with sharp-looking plates. The ground shakes as they move across the plain.

Turn the page.

"Let's go!" Jasmine says. "Look, there's a smaller one. Let's all put our hands on it and think of home."

Smaller is a relative term. The Stegosaurus still dwarfs even the largest bison. If it gets spooked, you'll all be prehistoric pancakes.

To go ahead with the plan, turn to page 68.
To keep your distance, turn to page 71.

There's no time for rest. You strike out across the open plain. You come upon a river. It has carved deep cliffs in the landscape, leaving a steep, rocky bank.

"This is limestone," Eduardo says. "There might be caves. It could be a perfect spot to take shelter."

You spend the rest of the day searching for caves. Jasmine spots one halfway down a particularly steep cliff.

"That would be the perfect place to take shelter," Eduardo says. "But I'm not sure we could make the climb. Falling to our deaths isn't really any better than becoming a dinosaur snack."

"I'm willing to take my chances," Jasmine says. They both look to you.

To look for a better spot, turn to page 75.
To make the climb, turn to page 76.

The rocks don't offer much shelter. But at least you don't have to worry about falling out of a tree in your sleep. The three of you collapse to the ground, backs against the rocks. You're all exhausted. You can only hope you'll be safe here.

After the sun sets, a full moon shines down on the open plains. A scratching sound from the ferns sets your heart racing. You scan the horizon, searching for the shape of some great predator. But there's nothing. Then, out of the brush, something emerges. It's a dinosaur, but it's tiny—not much bigger than a house cat. You let out a breath.

"Hey little guy," you call out softly.

The little dinosaur locks its gaze on you. It takes a careful step forward. Then another. You watch with curiosity. That curiosity turns to terror as another emerges. And another.

Turn the page.

Soon, you're surrounded by the tiny beasts. One of them seemed cute. But dozens of them suddenly are terrifying. And when they charge, you have nowhere to run.

The little dinosaurs, which Eduardo would have told you were Compsognathuses, are lightning-quick, strong, and ferocious. As you face your doom, you can't help but feel cheated. At least if you were going to be eaten by a dinosaur, it could have been a big, terrible lizard. Dying at the hands of a pack of little ones just seems so unfair.

THE END

To follow another path, turn to page 11.
To learn more about the Jurassic Period, turn to page 103.

You won't be a part of this. Maybe if you just strike off in the opposite direction, they'll see that you're right. They'll follow you.

But they don't. And by the time you have second thoughts, they've disappeared into the prairie. They're gone, and you're alone.

You're faster and more efficient on your own. You find eggs and seeds to eat. A rushing brook gives you fresh water.

Days turn to weeks. The flat plains slowly give way to rocky land. It provides plenty of nooks and crannies that offer shelter. As you travel, you see countless dinosaurs. Great herds of armored Stegosauruses and giant Brachiosauruses graze on ferns and brush. You steer clear of the terrible Allosauruses, Ceratosauruses, and other meat eaters.

You make your home on a cliff along a rushing river. You fish. You even learn to set traps for small mammals and dinosaurs. Somehow you survive and grow old. Your hair slowly turns gray.

One day, when you're foraging, you spot something far in the distance. It's a *human*!

You run. You shout. It must be one of your friends, after all these years. But the person is too far away. He or she doesn't see you. By the time you reach the ridge, there's no one there.

You'd assumed Jasmine and Eduardo had died. But now your heart is filled with hope. You will not rest until you find whomever it was you saw in the distance. Maybe you won't have to spend your final years alone after all.

THE END

To follow another path, turn to page 11.
To learn more about the Jurassic Period, turn to page 103.

You've come this far, why stop now? You take a deep breath and follow Jasmine. Eduardo is right behind you.

The Stegosaurus is munching on some low ferns. If it notices you approaching, it doesn't seem to mind. Now that you're close to it, the size of the beast truly astounds you. It's more than twice your height, and as long as a bus. Jasmine places her hand on the animal's huge rear leg. It doesn't stir. Eduardo does the same. They both look back at you, waiting.

"Here goes nothing," you mutter under your breath, reaching out your hand.

The animal's hide is rough and leathery. It's warmer than you expected. You close your eyes and imagine home. You concentrate on places and people, imagining what it's like to live in your time.

Turn the page.

Suddenly you feel a familiar sense of dizziness. You start to fall and then pass out. When you wake, you're on the floor of the museum. The Stegosaurus skeleton towers over you.

Your mind is fuzzy. You have strange memories of a distant place and strange adventures. Jasmine and Eduardo sit up and rub their eyes.

"Did that really just happen?" you ask.

The three of you catch up with your class in the Ancient Egypt exhibit. By the time you leave the museum, you've almost forgotten all of it, like a dream fading away with morning light.

Was it real? As the years pass, you're not sure. Maybe it was your imagination. Or just maybe, you had one of the strangest adventures of all time.

THE END

To follow another path, turn to page 11.
To learn more about the Jurassic Period, turn to page 103.

"This is a bad idea," you say, backing away.

As you move, you stumble over a rock and let out a yelp. The sound spooks the Stegosaurus. It lumbers forward. Eduardo tries to dodge the beast, but it swats him with its massive tail.

The blow sends Eduardo's limp body flying. Jasmine screams. The dinosaur whips its tail again, now in her direction. You can only watch in horror.

Just like that, you're all alone. The herd moves on, leaving your friends lifeless on the ground.

You never do go home. Somehow you survive into old age. Your life in the Jurassic is difficult and lonely. There are times you almost wish the Stegosaurus had gotten you too.

THE END

To follow another path, turn to page 11.
To learn more about the Jurassic Period, turn to page 103.

Your hand is throbbing.

"I think I might throw up," you say with a grimace. "I need to rest."

You quickly drift off to sleep. You awaken with a start. Jasmine is screaming. Eduardo is tugging on your shirt. The sight of a towering dinosaur looming over you reminds you very quickly where . . . and when . . . you are.

"Allosaurus!" Eduardo shouts.

Your friends are running, but the Allosaurus is gaining on them.

"Ed! Jasmine!" you shout.

Without even thinking about it, you rush after them, toward the dinosaur.

"Hey!" you shout at the beast, waving your arms in the air.

Turn the page.

You just want to distract it long enough to let your friends escape. But then the dinosaur turns on you. It covers the open ground between you with blinding speed. There's nowhere to hide. It's too fast. As you frantically try to zig and zag out of its path, you can feel its hot breath. Its jaws open wide. It strikes.

You've given your life for your friends. You just hope they took the chance you gave them to get away.

THE END

To follow another path, turn to page 11.
To learn more about the Jurassic Period, turn to page 103.

Ed is right. The climb down might be more dangerous than taking your chances up here.

"Keep going," you decide. "If there's one cave, there should be more."

The sun dips low in the sky as you search.

"There's just nothing here," Jasmine says with exasperation. "We're running out of time."

Dusk turns to dark. When the predators come, Eduardo can't even tell you what the horse-sized dinosaurs are. There's not enough time. The pack surrounds you, cutting off any avenue of escape.

You only wish you'd tried to take shelter in the cave. Three humans, exposed on the open plains of the Jurassic at night, never had a chance.

THE END

To follow another path, turn to page 11.
To learn more about the Jurassic Period, turn to page 103.

The climb is treacherous. But so is your current situation. Jasmine lowers herself down, grasping plant roots for support, until she reaches the small opening. Then she disappears inside. A minute later she sticks out her head, smiling.

"It's perfect!" she says. "Come on down."

You follow her route, almost slipping once and tumbling to your death. But you hold on, and so does Eduardo. You collapse into a cozy cave, just the right size for the three of you.

"Welcome to our new home," Jasmine says.

The cave is damp and narrow. But you'll be safe from predators here.

"We'll use those roots to make a ladder," Jasmine says. "We can go down to fish and up to forage for food. We can survive here!"

All thoughts of trying to get home have disappeared. The reality of your situation has sunk in. The Jurassic is where you live now. You're just glad you have your friends with you. You don't think you could make it alone. Together, you have a chance to survive.

THE END

To follow another path, turn to page 11.
To learn more about the Jurassic Period, turn to page 103.

CHAPTER 4

INTO THE WETLANDS

"Let's go that way," you say, pointing to the wetlands. "I read once that if you're lost, you should follow the water."

It doesn't take long before you begin to question your choice. The ground here is damp and muddy. The deeper you go into the wetlands, the more difficult it is to move. Large, biting insects swarm you. They remind you of horseflies, but they're at least twice as big.

You follow a shallow river to where it joins a much larger river. Eduardo gasps at the size of it.

"This river must be as big as the Amazon," he says. "If we follow it, it should empty into the ocean somewhere."

Turn the page.

You all agree that the resources of the ocean and its coastline might offer your best chance at survival.

"But how will we get there?" Jasmine asks. "Walking is so slow. We should make a raft."

"Hmm," Eduardo mutters, shaking his head. "A river like that is going to be filled with predators. I'm not sure it's a great idea to try rafting down it."

"The land route isn't safe either," you say. "We don't know what sort of creatures live here."

Jasmine swats at one of the flies as it bites her on the arm. "These bugs alone might eat us alive if we walk."

To build a raft, go to the next page.
To continue on foot, turn to page 84.

"We can't keep slogging through this swampy muck," you decide. "That river will carry us where we need to go. It's worth the risk."

With that, the three of you set out building a raft. Jasmine quickly takes charge of the project. She's always been good at building things. You gather sticks and logs while Eduardo collects vines to tie them together. You carry the raft to the river's bank and launch. Jasmine uses a long stick to push the raft out into the current, while you and Eduardo use makeshift oars to steer. Soon, you're cruising down the current, watching the prehistoric world go by.

After about an hour, you see a sight that takes your breath away. A dinosaur stands at the river's edge, drinking. It raises its head and roars at you. "It's a young Allosaurus!" Eduardo says with glee. "Magnificent!"

Turn the page.

You lift your phone to take a picture. Just as you do, something bursts out of the water near the shoreline. It's an enormous crocodile! The monster is almost as long as a bus. It rises up out of the water, grabbing the young Allosaurus in its massive jaws. The dinosaur screams as it struggles, but it doesn't stand a chance. The croc drags it into the water, which churns red and bubbles for several seconds as the struggle continues. Then, suddenly, the water is eerily still.

You're speechless. You can't shake the image of the giant croc. Where there's one, there must be more. One could be beneath you right now.

To continue on the water, turn to page 88.

To steer to the opposite shore and get away from crocodile-infested waters, turn to page 99.

"Let's keep moving on foot," you suggest. "We'll see how it goes. We can always change our minds if it's not going well."

The three of you trudge through the swamp, often wading through waist-deep water. You detour away from the river bank when Eduardo spots a strip of higher, dryer land. It's there that you spot a nest. It's a huge bowl of mud, nestled near some tree roots. And it's filled with eggs. Enormous eggs.

"Could be supper," Jasmine suggests.

"I'd hate to run into whatever laid those eggs, though," Eduardo replies.

To leave the nest alone, go to the next page.
To try to gather some eggs, turn to page 90.

"Whatever laid those eggs could be close by," you say, backing away. "No, I think we'll leave those eggs right where they are."

You continue, following the river as it meanders through the swamp. Your feet stick in the mud with every step. Your legs are getting tired.

You notice some giant footprints in the wet ground. It almost looks like something bulldozed a path through this part of the swamp.

You hear the animal before you see it. Its low groan sends shivers down your spine. When you finally catch sight of it, though, Eduardo says you don't have to be afraid.

"It's a Diplodocus!" he says with excitement, "A plant eater."

Turn the page.

In fact, it's not just one. As you draw closer, you see a dozen or more of the huge dinosaurs, feasting on the plants that grow here. Their long, narrow tails trail behind them as they crash through the brush. The herd moves slowly along the river bank—in the same direction you want to go.

"We should go around them," Eduardo says.

"Why?" Jasmine asks. "They don't seem to care about us. They're going in our direction. Let's just join the herd."

"Are you crazy? These things may not care about us, but they'd crush us in a heartbeat if we get too close!"

To go around the herd, turn to page 92.
To join the herd, turn to page 94.

With a gulp, you decide to stay on your raft. Danger is everywhere. You're no safer on land than you are on the river. Luckily, you see no more signs of giant crocs. Within a day, you find what you're looking for—the ocean.

The river spills into the ocean in a massive delta. From your raft, you spot a sandy beach in the distance. You use your oars to steer ashore.

It's perfect. The sea gently laps the shore. There are no signs of large predators, aside from the washed-up skeleton of a truly massive shark.

"This is a place we can live," Eduardo says confidently.

You use small logs and driftwood to build a shelter just off the beach. You fish for food and gather edible plants. Days turn into weeks. Weeks turn into months.

Life is hard. You endure terrible storms, food shortages, and illness. But somehow you make it. You and your friends carve out a life.

"This just isn't enough," Jasmine decides one day. "We need to move on and explore. What's the point of living in the Jurassic if we can't see everything? Who knows, we might even find a way home."

You try to change her mind, but she's set in her decision. She's leaving. Eduardo refuses. He's staying. Like it or not, your little group is going to split up.

To stay on the beach with Eduardo, turn to page 96.
To explore the world with Jasmine, turn to page 101.

You're not going to survive long unless you eat something. You scan the ground for any sign of whatever laid those eggs, but you don't see anything.

"Here goes nothing," you say as you carefully approach the nest.

The eggs are oblong, more oval than a chicken egg, and much bigger. As you scoop one up, it feels almost soft to the touch. You tuck it under one arm like a football, then scoop up another. As you turn around, you hear a rustling from the trees above.

"Look out!" Eduardo calls.

Just then something massive drops from the trees. It's a snake! You once saw a giant anaconda at the zoo. This massive creature makes it seem tiny.

The snake wraps itself around you, coiling its body around and around. Eduardo and Jasmine try to save you, but they can't pry the snake loose. It starts to squeeze. The air rushes from your lungs. You hear the sound of your ribs cracking. Then everything goes black.

THE END

To follow another path, turn to page 11.
To learn more about the Jurassic Period, turn to page 103.

Ed is right. Even plant-eating dinosaurs of this size are a threat. You'll have to find another way.

You swing around the herd, putting some distance between you and the giant Diplodocuses. You're feeling good about your choice until you see a different kind of dinosaur—a meat-eating Ceratosaurus. It looks a little like the T. rexes you've seen in movies, walking upright on two hind legs. Razor-sharp teeth gleam from its open jaws.

The Ceratosaurus is big, fast, and hungry. You run as fast as you can, but it's not fast enough.

In the last moment before it snatches you up, you shout, "Keep running!"

Maybe your friends will escape your terrible fate.

THE END

To follow another path, turn to page 11.
To learn more about the Jurassic Period, turn to page 103.

"These guys are huge. Predators are going to keep their distance," you decide. "Let's take our chances with the herd."

The herd moves slowly along the bank. You stay close, and no predators come near. The dinosaurs mostly ignore you. They seem content to let you tag along.

Several days pass. After about a week with the herd, you head out in search of food. That's when you see something remarkable. You come upon a still pool of crystal-clear water. Thinking it might be a spring, you approach it. What you see beneath the surface takes your breath away. The reflection in the pool is home! You can see familiar plants, roads, and even buildings in the reflection. Could this be some portal back to your time? Your heart races with excitement.

"Hey!" you shout. "Come here!"

"Could it be a way home?" Ed asks.

You do the only thing you can. You dive into the cold water. When you return to the surface, everything has changed. You're back in your own time. Soaking wet, the three of you trudge through familiar plants and trees until you come to a highway. Your city is in the distance.

"What will we tell people?" Jasmine asks.

You've been asking yourself the same question. No one will believe you. That's when you remember your phone.

"If my memory card is still good, I've got some photographs that are going to make us famous," you say with a smile.

THE END

To follow another path, turn to page 11.
To learn more about the Jurassic Period, turn to page 103.

"This is the only place I've felt even a little bit safe since we came here," you tell Jasmine. "How can we leave it?"

She just shakes her head. She's determined to go off alone, and you can't stop her. You and Eduardo watch as she disappears around a bend in the shoreline. You're afraid you'll never see her again.

Life on the beach grows routine. You do the same things to survive, day after day. Your blazing campfire usually keeps the dinosaurs away.

Years pass. One day, Eduardo goes to collect wood for the fire. He doesn't return. You search for your friend but find no trace. He may have fallen prey to an Allosaurus, Ceratosaurus, or some other predator.

Turn the page.

You're all alone. Life was hard and repetitive even when you had company. Now, all alone, it's unbearable. You fall into depression. You stop maintaining your campfire. And the predators notice. When a pack of dog-sized dinosaurs strikes, you try climbing a small tree. But with a CRACK, the tree's trunk snaps. As you crash to the ground, you know what awaits. The small dinosaurs are about to get a taste of the future.

THE END

To follow another path, turn to page 11.
To learn more about the Jurassic Period, turn to page 103.

With monsters like that lurking below the muddy water, there's no way you can stay on this little raft.

"Let's get to land," you say.

The others nod their heads in agreement. You steer your raft to the other shore, far from where you saw the giant croc. It feels good to step back onto land. It's not so swampy here. You've floated into rockier, drier land.

For the next two days, you make your way on foot, drinking from small streams and eating mushrooms and seeds. Eduardo gets sick first. His stomach is cramping badly, and he can't keep anything down. You and Jasmine soon suffer from the same illness.

"Probably something in the water," Eduardo moans. "A bacteria or a parasite."

Turn the page.

Within a day, Eduardo is delirious. You're all burning up with a terrible fever. You suffer from extreme chills. There's nowhere to go for help and no one coming to your aid. You thought meat-eating dinosaurs were the biggest danger in this time period, but it turns out the microscopic life in the Jurassic is every bit as deadly.

THE END

To follow another path, turn to page 11.
To learn more about the Jurassic Period, turn to page 103.

You can't let Jasmine go alone. Eduardo has everything he needs to survive here. You pack some dried fish, and head out with Jasmine along the coast. As you round a bend, you take one last long look at Eduardo. Will you ever see him again?

You and Jasmine see amazing things. You escape packs of small, speedy theropods. You are nearly swallowed up by a sinkhole. Jasmine rides an Apatosaurus. You travel the world, seeing creatures that will one day be lost to history.

It's the adventure of a lifetime, but through it all, you never stop dreaming of home and your family. You'll never see them again. You understand that now. One day, you'll return to the beach. You just hope Eduardo is still there to welcome you.

THE END

To follow another path, turn to page 11.
To learn more about the Jurassic Period, turn to page 103.

CHAPTER 5

THE JURASSIC PERIOD

The Jurassic Period was at the heart of the Mesozoic Era. This era is known as the Age of Reptiles. The Jurassic spanned about 55 million years, starting at the end of the Triassic Period about 201 million years ago.

The Jurassic Period was the time when dinosaurs rose up to dominate life on Earth. Giant Diplodocus, measuring 100 feet long, ate plant life. Deadly Allosaurus hunted small prey. Spiky Stegosaurus roamed the land in large herds. Pterosaurs soared through the skies. Marine reptiles such as plesiosaurs swam in the seas. Meanwhile, the earliest birds appeared during this time, having evolved from dinosaurs.

The Jurassic was marked by major changes in Earth's geology. It saw the breakup of the supercontinent Pangaea, which split into two main landmasses, called Laurasia and Gondwanaland. The opening of seaways about 145 million years ago marked the end of the Jurassic and the beginning of a new period, the Cretaceous.

Dinosaurs and other reptiles continued to rule the planet during that period. It ended about 65 million years ago with a mass extinction that wiped out the dinosaurs and many other life forms on Earth. Scientists have found evidence of a large asteroid strike that likely caused this extinction. It knocked reptiles from their rule and paved the way for an age of more adaptable mammals to begin.

TIMELINE

252 million years ago •••

Paleozoic Era
time of ancient life

Mesozoic Era
time of dinosaurs

251 ••••••••••••••••••200
million years ago   million years ago
TRIASSIC PERIOD

200 ••••••••••••••••••••••••••••
million years ago
JURASSIC PERIOD

252 MILLION YEARS AGO
A mass extinction marks the end of the Paleozoic Era, sparking a rapid change in animal and plant life. The Mesozoic Era begins, with the first of its three periods, the Triassic. The age of reptiles begins.

210-200 MILLION YEARS AGO
The first mammals appear.

180 MILLION YEARS AGO
The Atlantic Ocean and Indian Ocean form as the supercontinent Pangaea breaks apart.

201 MILLION YEARS AGO
The supercontinent Pangaea begins to break up, causing rapid changes to the planet's climate and setting off a large extinction event. This marks the end of the Triassic Period and the beginning of the Jurassic. The planet's climate is warm and wet, supporting a wide variety of life.

230-220 MILLION YEARS AGO
The first dinosaurs appear.

·· ·65 million years ago

Cenozoic Era
time of mammals

·· · · · · · · · ·146
million years ago

145 ·· ·65
million years ago   million years ago

CRETACEOUS PERIOD

65 MILLION YEARS AGO
A massive asteroid strike drastically changes Earth's climate. Large reptiles such as dinosaurs are unable to adapt to the rapidly changing conditions, leading to a mass extinction. The Cretaceous Period, and the Mesozoic Era, end. The Cenozoic Era begins. It is the Age of Mammals.

145 MILLION YEARS AGO
The Jurassic Period ends, giving way to the Cretaceous Period. Dinosaurs such as Tyrannosaurus rex and Triceratops roam the Earth during the Cretaceous.

150 MILLION YEARS AGO
Archaeopteryx appears in the fossil record. Among the many kinds of feathered dinosaurs, scientists recognize it as the earliest bird.

80 MILLION YEARS AGO
North America separates from Europe, completing the breakup of Pangaea.

OTHER PATHS TO EXPLORE

>>> Human beings did not exist during the Jurassic Period, but mammals did. What would life have been like for these small mammals, living in a world of giant reptiles? How do you think they survived?

>>> What if dinosaurs and other animals of the Jurassic were transported into modern times? How would human beings treat them? Would we hunt them to extinction? Put them in zoos? Or would they adapt and once again rule the planet?

>>> If you could go back in time and live during the Jurassic Period, what type of environment would you want to live in? How would you survive?

READ MORE

Braun, Eric. *Can You Survive the Cretaceous?* North Mankato, MN: Capstone Press, 2020.

DK Publishing. *First Dinosaur Encyclopedia*. New York: DK Publishing, 2016.

Lee, Sally. *Allosaurus*. North Mankato, MN: Capstone Press, 2015.

INTERNET SITES

Dinosaurs: National Geographic Kids
kids.nationalgeographic.com/explore/nature/dinosaurs/

Jurassic Landscape
www.nationalgeographic.com/science/prehistoric-world/jurassic/

The Jurassic Period
www.activewild.com/the-jurassic-period/

GLOSSARY

Cretaceous Period (kri-TAY-shus PIHR-ee-uhd)—the third period of the Mesozoic Era; the Cretaceous Period was from about 145 to 65 million years ago

evolve (i-VAHLV)—to change gradually, especially concerning animals or plants

extinct (ik-STINGKT)—no longer living; an extinct animal is one that has died out, with no more of its kind

fossil (FAH-suhl)—the remains of an ancient plant or animal that have hardened into rock; also the preserved tracks or outline of an ancient organism

herbivore (HUR-buh-vor)—an animal that eats only plants

Jurassic Period (jur-ASS-ik PIHR-ee-uhd)—the second period of the Mesozoic Era, lasting from about 200 to 146 million years ago, when birds first appeared

Pangaea (pan-JEE-uh)—a landmass believed to have once connected all Earth's continents together

predator (PRED-uh-tur)—an animal that hunts other animals for food

Triassic Period (try-ASS-ik PIRH-ee-uhd)—the earliest period of the Mesozoic Era, lasting from about 251 to 200 million years ago, when dinosaurs first appeared

BIBLIOGRAPHY

Britannica: Jurassic Period
www.britannica.com/science/Jurassic-Period

Dinosaur Timeline Gallery
www.prehistory.com/timeline/jurassic.htm

The Jurassic Period
www.nationalgeographic.com/science/prehistoric-world/
jurassic/

Jurassic Period Facts
www.livescience.com/28739-jurassic-period.html

Paul, Gregory S. *The Princeton Field Guide to Dinosaurs:
Second Edition*. Princeton, NJ: Princeton University
Press, 2016.

INDEX